For Kirsty, Rory and Jamie
L.G.
For my Book Pen Pals at Glebe Primary Year 1
L.H.

8817

8817

WILDFLOWER
SEED MIX

Bee Friendly

39

EGMONT
We bring stories to life

First published in Great Britain 2020 by Egmont UK Limited,
2 Minster Court, 10th Floor, London EC3R 7BB
www.egmont.co.uk

Text copyright © Louise Greig 2020
Illustrations copyright © Laura Hughes 2020
Louise Greig and Laura Hughes have asserted their moral rights.
ISBN 978 1 4052 8781 4

Stay safe online. Egmont is not responsible for content hosted by third parties.

Egmont takes its responsibility to the planet and its inhabitants very seriously.
We aim to use papers from well-managed forests run by responsible suppliers.

remember the honey!

The Bear Who Did

382438

ADMIT ONE

382438

LOUISE GREIG • LAURA HUGHES

This is the bear who **did not** steal the honey.

This is the bear
who did.

This is the bear **who did**
not find it **funny**.

This is the bear
who did.

This is the bear who **searched** for the honey.

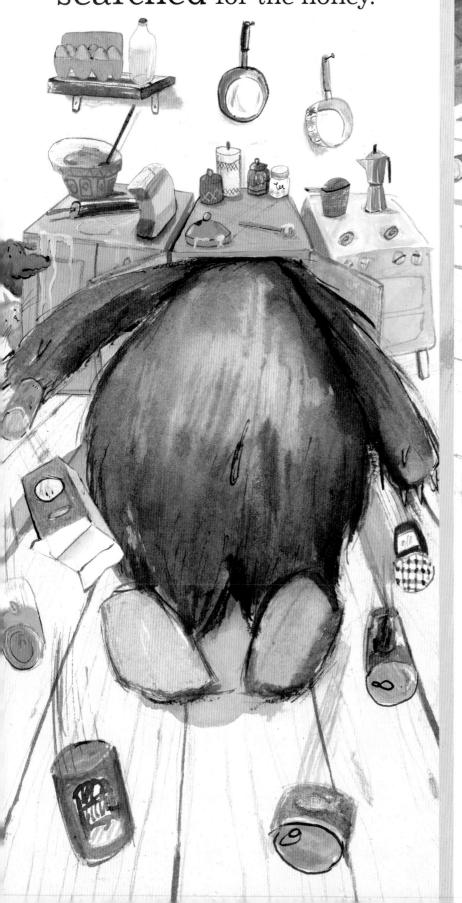

This is the bear **who hid**.

This is the bear who **roared** for the honey:

"Where is the bear who did?"

This is the **roar** that **rattled** the door.

This is the milk that **tipped**.

This is the flour that **poured** in a shower.

This is the bear who **slipped**.

These are the eyes full of surprise.

This is the cat who crept.

This is the glance.

This is the chance.

This is the dog who leapt . . .

This is the bear

who flew through the air.

These are
the walls
that shook.

This is the clock that

ticked

and tocked

and rocked

and rocked . . .

Uh-oh . . .

Don't look!

This is the bear.

"This is not fair!"

These are the wings that flapped.

These are the bees high in the trees.
This is the branch that **snapped**.

This is the bear full of despair.

This is the rain that poured.

"HELP!"

These are the paws.

This is the noise.

This is the bear who **snored**.

This is the elk who heard the "HELP!"
This is the beaver too.

This is the fox.

These are the knocks.

"Is there anything we can do?"

This is the help
that followed the elk.

This is the floor that creaked.

This is the squeeze that upset the bees.

B U Z Z Z Z Z Z Z!

This is the help that shrieked!

"Eeeek!"

"Ouch!"

"Run!"

These are the thumps.

These are the jumps.

This is the house
that shook.

This is the pear.

This is
the bear.
Uh-oh!

Don't look!

This is the bear who slid on her tummy into
the bear who hid. This is the bear who said,

"Don't mention honey!"

This is the bear
who did.

"WANT SOME?"